CAN I CATCH IT LIKE A COLD?
COPING WITH A PARENT'S DEPRESSION

Presented by the Centre for Addiction and Mental Health

Illustrated by JOE WEISSMANN

TUNDRA BOOKS

Published in Canada by Tundra Books,
75 Sherbourne Street, Toronto, Ontario M5A 2P9

Published in the United States by Tundra Books of Northern New York,
P.O. Box 1030, Plattsburgh, New York 12901

Library of Congress Control Number: 2009920670

Library and Archives Canada Cataloguing in Publication
Can I catch it like a cold? : coping with a parent's depression /
Centre for Addiction and Mental Health ; Joe Weissmann, illustrator.
(Coping series)
Includes bibliographical references.
ISBN 978-0-88776-956-6
1. Depression, Mental–Juvenile fiction. 2. Parents – Mental health–Juvenile fiction.
3. Children of depressed persons –Juvenile fiction. I. Weissmann, Joe, 1947-
II. Centre for Addiction and Mental Health III. Series: Coping
RC537.C35 2009   jC813'.6   C2009-900362-7

We acknowledge the financial support of the Government of Canada through the Book Publishing Industry Development Program (BPIDP) and that of the Government of Ontario through the Ontario Media Development Corporation's Ontario Book Initiative. We further acknowledge the support of the Canada Council for the Arts and the Ontario Arts Council for our publishing program.

ONTARIO ARTS COUNCIL
CONSEIL DES ARTS DE L'ONTARIO

camh
Centre for Addiction and Mental Health
Centre de toxicomanie et de santé mentale

A Pan American Health Organization /
World Health Organization Collaborating Centre

Medium: Watercolor
Development: Susan Rosenstein, CAMH; Kathy Lowinger, Tundra Books;
Lauren Bailey, Tundra Books; Jennifer Lum, Random House; Joe Weissmann

Printed and bound in Canada

1 2 3 4 5 6   14 13 12 11 10 09

ACKNOWLEDGMENTS

Centre for Addiction and Mental Health Project Team
Susan Rosenstein, MA, Publishing Developer and Product Developer; Christina Bartha, MSW, Administrative Director, Mood and Anxiety Disorders Service, Child Psychiatry and Addiction Programs; Lynn Oldershaw, PhD, Staff Psychologist, Child Psychiatry Program; Patricia Merka, RN, BScN, Dipl.TCPP, Staff Nurse, Mood and Anxiety Disorders Service, Child, Youth and Family Program, CAMH; Irfan A. Mian, MD, FRCPC, DABPN, Clinical Head, Mood and Anxiety Disorders Service and Psychotic Disorders Service, Child, Youth and Family Program, CAMH

Special thanks to the following people who reviewed early versions of this book and provided invaluable insight and feedback:
Tatyana Barankin, MD, FRCPC, DCP
Head, Continuing Medical Education for the Division of Child Psychiatry, Child Psychiatry Program, CAMH
Assistant Professor of Psychiatry, Department of Psychiatry, University of Toronto

Nili Benazon, PhD
Research Scientist, Society Women and Health, CAMH, Sunnybrook & Women's College Health Sciences Centre
Assistant Professor, Department of Psychiatry, University of Toronto

Marshall Korenblum, MD, FRCP(C), Dip. Child. Psych.,
Psychiatrist-in-Chief, Hincks-Dellcrest Centre for Children
Associate Professor, Faculty of Medicine, University of Toronto

Katherina Manassis, MD, FRCPC
Staff Psychiatrist, Mood and Anxiety Disorders Service, Joint Child Psychiatry Program, CAMH and Hospital for Sick Children
Associate Professor of Psychiatry, University of Toronto

Mark Sanford, MD, MBChB
Head, Mood and Anxiety Disorders Service, Joint Child Psychiatry Program, CAMH and Hospital for Sick Children

Parents with knowledge of depression, including Pauline Head, also reviewed the book and provided additional insight.

I was worried and I was angry. All my dad ever wanted to do was sleep. He seemed lazy. He didn't go to work anymore. He stopped playing guitar in his band. Whenever Sparky brought his ball for a game of fetch, Dad would just pat him on the head.

One night, Mom worked late. Dad stayed in his room. I had a bowl of ice cream for dinner.

When Mom got home, she saw the empty ice-cream bowl and asked Dad why he hadn't heated up the soup she'd made. They had another big argument.

When Mom came to tuck me in, she could tell that I
had been crying.

"What's wrong?" she asked.

"It's my fault that Dad acts the way he does." I hadn't
meant to say anything, but somehow it just came out.

"It's not your fault. It's nobody's fault. Dad acts the way he does because of depression. Depression is something that happens with the brain. People with depression may feel really sad and think or act differently than when they are well."

The next morning, Dad didn't eat breakfast with us. "The Secords will take you to your soccer game after school," said Mom.

"I don't want to go. I never get a goal." I didn't feel like eating my toast.

"I can see you're feeling discouraged, dear, but try to go anyway," she said. "For your first year of soccer, you're really good."

"Why can't Dad take me? He never watches me play."

"Your dad doesn't feel well right now, Alex. Let him sleep. Maybe he'll feel better when you come home from school."

When I got home from school, I heard Dad in the bathroom. Great! Now he could take me to the game and watch me play. Maybe I would score a goal!

I put on my uniform and went to look for Dad. He was sitting on his bed, rocking back and forth and crying a little.

I patted him. I didn't know what else to do. "I'm sorry, Dad. About the ice cream. About everything."

Though the Secords cheered me on, I felt bad and I played bad. I wanted to run home and stay in my room.

After the game, I was waiting for Mrs. Secord to get the car when Anna, one of the refs, rode by. The chain came off her bike. She kicked it, but that didn't help. I put the chain back on for her. "My dad's good at fixing cars and things," I explained. "He showed me how to take care of my bike."

"Where's your dad these days?"

"My dad is sick sometimes. He has depression." I don't know why I told her that. I don't like to talk about it. What she said next surprised me.

"My mom does, too." She got back on her bike. "You'd do better at soccer if you went after the ball more. You're a good player, but you can't wait for the ball to come to you. You have to go for it. Next week before the game, if you want, I'll show you what I mean."

The next week, Mrs. Secord dropped me off early, and Anna showed me how to kick the ball better. When we stopped to rest, she told me about her mom. Her mom works in a bank.

"Why didn't she lose her job, like my dad did?" I asked. "He was a police officer. He was afraid they'd fire him, so he quit."

"They wouldn't fire him if he got help. He could get better." She rolled the ball back and forth.

"Can you really get better?"

"Sure."

I felt better just talking to Anna. It felt so good to talk to someone about big worries.

"Anna," I asked, "why is my dad so tired and angry and sad all the time? How does he feel when he's depressed? What's going on in his head?"

"When people are depressed, it's hard for them to enjoy things like watching their kids play sports. My mom never watched me play soccer either. A person with depression can feel like crying and can be tired all the time, and they can sleep a lot, too." I nodded. Boy, she knew all about my dad.

"Is that why Dad doesn't play the guitar or throw the ball for the dog or even get out of bed some days?"

"I think so. When my mom was sick, she couldn't think for a long time about any one thing. The sickness makes it hard for some people to think the way they do when they feel better. She had to take time off work. She couldn't concentrate on all those big numbers, and that's not good when you work at a bank!" We smiled.

"Mom says Dad's let himself go. He hardly shaves or showers. Did your mom act like that?"

Anna looked away. "Depression makes different people think and act in different ways. My mom worried a lot and got mad all the time. 'Do your homework! Turn off the TV!' Sometimes she said mean things. I thought she didn't like me."

"And then she got better?"

"Well, she got better and then sick again. She was even in the hospital a couple of times. It gave her a chance to rest, talk about her feelings, and try some medicines. By the time she came home, her psychiatrist – a kind of 'feelings' doctor – had found a medication that helped her to get well. Now Mom sees a therapist, who talks with her and helps her find ways to stay healthy. It works. It may take awhile, but they can find out what works for your dad. I started seeing a therapist, too."

"But you weren't sick."

"No. But I needed to share my feelings about Mom. I learned that she didn't mean to get angry and that she always loves me, even when she's sick. The most important thing I learned was that it wasn't my fault. I didn't make her get depressed. It just happened. It felt so good not to feel guilty about it." Anna stood up and wiped the grass off her shorts.

"My mom asked me if I wanted to talk to somebody and I told her no." I remembered the argument we had had.

"You know, you can't help your father feel better, but you can help yourself. I did. I learned as much as I could about depression. The more I know, the better I feel about it and about me. Now, let's see if all that kicking practice helps your game."

I played my best game all season, though I didn't get a goal!

After dinner, I talked to my mom about Anna's mother. When Dad came downstairs, Mom told him what we'd been talking about. He was glad to hear what I had learned.

"Your teacher can arrange for any kid who has a problem to talk to the counselor at school," Mom said. "I'll call her tomorrow."

I went to bed happy and relieved.

I was nervous when I went to see the counselor, Miss Yee. First, we talked about school and soccer. Then I told her about my dad. I asked her what I really wanted to know. "What causes depression? How does it start?"

"Everybody gets sad at times. But when it's really bad and lasts a long time, it's depression. And some people get depressed more easily than others," she explained.

"Many things can cause depression. And what causes it in one person can be different from what causes it in another. The symptoms can come from big changes, like when someone they love dies. Or maybe they lose their job or have a bad accident. They could be feeling a lot of stress. Or maybe the person gets another sickness that causes depression."

"But none of those things happened to my dad," I said.

"Sometimes we don't even know why a person gets depressed. The symptoms – that means the way they act – just come," she said. "The important thing is to know that it is not your fault."

That was what Anna had said!

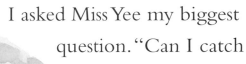

I asked Miss Yee my biggest question. "Can I catch it, like a cold?"

"No, there isn't a germ that causes depression, like with a cold or the flu. You can't catch it from your dad."

"But will I get it?" I was still worried.

"No one knows if they will become depressed. If your parent has depression, you may get it, but it's also very likely that you won't."

"What can I do so I won't get depressed?" I didn't want to be sad.

"You're doing it right now!" she said. "Talking about problems and questions with your parents and other grown-ups, like me, can help you to feel better and deal with those problems."

"My dad makes me feel mad sometimes, or sad, or scared, and I don't know what to do."

"Many kids who have parents going through depression feel those things at times. And they may be afraid to talk about such feelings because they think their parents have too much to worry about already. Sometimes that's true, but parents usually want to hear about how you feel and what you worry about. They want to hear all about your life."

"What else can I do, other than talk about depression?"

"You can join clubs, play sports, hang out with friends, and spend time with other adults who aren't depressed."

"Thanks, Miss Yee." Anna was right. I felt much better.

"There are lots of people who work with kids to help them with their feelings. You can check in with me while your dad's going through this, or you can talk to a psychologist – another kind of 'feelings' doctor – or to your own doctor."

The next week, I went to talk to Dr. Bean, a psychologist. I tried not to laugh at his name. I asked him the same question I had asked Anna. "Do you think my dad will ever get better?"

"Most people with depression who get help do get better," he said. "If the depression comes back, and it sometimes does, doctors can treat it again."

That made me feel better. "My dad's in treatment, but I don't really know what that means."

"There are two ways to treat depression."

"One is to find pills that help the person's brain to work better. The pills help them to think, feel, and act the way they did before they got sick. The other way is for the person with depression to talk to a therapist like a psychologist, a psychiatrist, a nurse, or a social worker."

"My dad sees a psychiatrist."

Dr. Bean nodded. "Your dad's learning ways to help him get through this difficult time – new ways to cope." I thought about all the things my dad had liked to do, like playing in his band, throwing balls for Sparky, and watching me play soccer.

Soccer season's nearly over now. Dad's feeling better.

His doctors are looking for the best kind of pill for him. All the talk therapy helps, too. He smiles more and there aren't as many arguments at home.

Things are going well with me, too. I scored a goal! I even scored it before Dad started coming to my games. I do what Anna said. I don't wait for the ball to come to me anymore. I go for it!

INFORMATION FOR ADULTS

The Centre for Addiction and Mental Health (CAMH) is one of the leading addiction and mental health organizations in North America, and it is Canada's largest mental health and addiction teaching hospital. CAMH provides outstanding clinical care, conducts groundbreaking research, provides expert training, develops innovative health promotion and prevention strategies, and influences public policy at all levels of government. CAMH also develops publications and resources for health professionals, clients, and the public, providing the most extensive and up-to-date information on topics that range from prevention to treatment of mental illness and addictions, and promoting best practices in the field.

TALKING ABOUT DEPRESSION

If there's a history of depression in your family, it's important that you know what depression is and how to treat it. If a parent has depression, it's crucial for your family to know what can protect children against depression or against feeling hopeless about the family situation.

Can I Catch It Like a Cold? provides helpful and easy-to-understand answers to children's most common questions, and it offers the parent, grandparent, teacher, mental health or addiction professional, or other concerned adult a tool to aid in talking with children about depression. Encouraging children to start talking about family issues related to depression is one of the most important things you can do for them.

Remember, when a family member has depression, the issues are complex. This book is not intended to replace professional help. Please get help from a professional.

WHY TALK ABOUT A PARENT'S DEPRESSION?

If the family doesn't talk openly about a parent's depression, it can become the big secret that is never discussed. When children don't get information, they often draw their own conclusions, and their ideas may be wrong or frightening. Some of their most common fears are that they are the cause of the disorder, they make it worse, they have the power to make the parent better, that the parent will go to hospital or die, or that the parent will never get better. Good communication within a family is related to a child's ability to make healthy, positive choices in difficult life situations, and it contributes to their resilience or ability to cope with adversity.

Children often understand more than you might think. They need to be able to ask questions, even though it's often hard for them to do so. And they need clear, concise, and age-appropriate answers. Research shows that if kids understand their parent's depression, they do better later in life. Children need to understand that they did not cause the depression, they can reach out to adults, they are not responsible for making the parent better, and that the parent's mood and behavior is no one's fault.

If your children are open to talking, this story can give you ways to explain depression. If your children are not open to talking, simply reading the story will let them know that the questions they think about are the same ones that other children have. Talking about their thoughts will likely help them to feel less alone and confused. Over time, they may feel better able to share their feelings.

You will likely find that, as the conversations develop, children will ask many "spin-off" questions or raise other concerns. It makes sense that when children hear someone is ill, they might fear that the person could die. Explain that depression does not stop the body from working, like a heart attack might. When people are depressed, they may at times feel so bad that they say "I want to die." This can be very scary for a child to hear. While we don't introduce the issue of suicide in this story, if a child does bring up the topic, or if it is a factor in their parent's life, the following are suggestions for addressing it:

- Explain that suicidal thoughts are one of many symptoms that
  someone with depression could have.

- Reassure your children about suicide or a parent's self-harming by
  ensuring they understand two things:

  1. The parent has never wanted to hurt or kill him or herself.
     (Say this only if it's true.)
  2. If the parent were to feel so bad that he or she wanted to die,
     a doctor, therapist, or someone else would help the parent to
     stop feeling that way.

Remember, encouraging children to start talking to you and others about depression is one of the most important things you can do for them.